RIMA'S REBELLION

MARGARITA ENGLE

RIMA'S REBELLION

COURAGE IN A TIME OF TYRANNY

 atheneum NEW YORK LONDON TORONTO SYDNEY NEW DELHI

atheneum

An imprint of Simon & Schuster Children's Publishing Division
1230 Avenue of the Americas, New York, New York 10020

Text © 2022 by Margarita Engle
Jacket illustration © 2022 by Carina Guevara
Jacket design by Rebecca Syracuse © 2022 by Simon & Schuster, Inc.

For information about special discounts for bulk purchases, please contact Simon & Schuster Special Sales at 1-866-506-1949 or business@simonandschuster.com.
The Simon & Schuster Speakers Bureau can bring authors to your live event. For more information or to book an event, contact the Simon & Schuster Speakers Bureau at 1-866-248-3049 or visit our website at www.simonspeakers.com.
Interior design by Rebecca Syracuse
The text for this book was set in Haboro and Core Circus.
Manufactured in the United States of America
First Edition
10 9 8 7 6 5 4 3 2 1
Library of Congress Cataloging-in-Publication Data
Names: Engle, Margarita, author.
Title: Rima's rebellion : courage in a time of tyranny / Margarita Engle.
Description: First edition. | New York : Atheneum Books for Young Readers, [2022] | Includes bibliographic references. | Audience: Ages 12 and Up. | Summary: In 1920s Cuba, Rima is bullied and shunned for her illegitimacy, but finds solace in riding her horse and forges unexpected friendships with others who share her dreams of freedom and suffrage. Includes historical note.
Identifiers: LCCN 2021005919 | ISBN 9781534486935 (hardcover) | ISBN 9781534486959 (ebook)
Subjects: CYAC: Novels in verse. | Family life—Cuba—Fiction. | Suffragists—Fiction. | Friendship—Fiction. | Cuba—History—1909-1933—Fiction. Classification: LCC PZ7.5.E54 Ri 2022 | DDC [Fic]—dc23
LC record available at https://lccn.loc.gov/2021005919

FOR ALL GIRLS,
BECAUSE YOU HAVE ALWAYS
DESERVED EQUAL RIGHTS

MAMBISA (Mahm-BEE-sah): A woman who served as an independence fighter or battlefield nurse during Cuba's three wars for freedom from Spain. Las mambisas traveled on horseback through densely forested wilderness. Their courage and perseverance were legendary. Some went on to become suffragists during peacetime, when women organized clubs to demand voting rights.

CONTENTS

PART ONE

REBELLION IS IN THE AIR

RIMA MARÍN
AGE 12
GUANABACOA, HAVANA, CUBA
1923

EL RODEO

During the lull between protests
we ride bareback
no bridle
or bit
no spurs
just silent messages
sent to our horses
through the pressure
of hands
knees
feet
weight
seat.

Balance
    is the magic
that helps us gallop
    side by side
as we ride
    in dazzling
formations:
    two loops
make a figure eight,
then pirouettes
and leaps
a horseback ballet

before finally—breathless
and exhilarated—we exit
the dusty arena
cheered on
by raucous
applause
for las feministas!

CHAIRS FOR WEARY WOMEN

Everyone is angry.
Students in the city seize the university.
War veterans denounce government corruption.
Women demand voting rights!

Chairs.
Such simple objects, yet somehow they feel huge
and complicated when Abuela and Mamá let me
help carry our gift
of smooth wooden seats
to exhausted store clerks
who have been standing
as rigidly and obediently as soldiers
day
after day
year
after year.

Chairs.
Such a quiet act of kindness
for hardworking women
whose stern male bosses
expect them to remain standing at attention,
never resting, not even during long
quiet moments
between customers.

Mamá says our chair-delivery protest
is a simple act of mercy for struggling women,
but storekeepers accuse us of behaving
like criminals.

That's why I plan to cling
to my own female reality
forever
never believing
false accusations
made by men.

PANIC

Rhythm
    is the power
    of hoofbeats.

Courage
    is the essence
    of triumph . . .

but bravery comes and goes, ebbs, then flows
like a tide on the shore of my turbulent
    childhood.

Until I learned the meaning
of the cruel word "bastarda,"
fear rarely defeated me.

Now, unless I'm on horseback,
sharing the height and strength
of my buckskin mare, any encounter
with an insult-shouting
man or boy
truly terrifies me.

There is no logical reason for these tidal waves
of anxiety
because I live with Abuela and Mamá,

no father,
brothers, or uncles,
so all I know of average families is what I hear
and see
at the blacksmith shop and around town,
where men command, women work,
and girls obey,
struggling to ignore boys
who hurl words
made of hatred.

¡Bastarda!
My breath fails.
I'm undecided between shame
and rage, a battle of emotions
that leaves me feeling as weak
and helpless
as a swirling feather
caught in a whirlpool
birdless.

A NATURAL CHILD

Those harsh insults
shake me so brutally
that I almost lose my balance
even while I cling to Ala's dark mane
with desperation, leaning forward
against her sweaty neck, pressing my face
to her muscles,
hoping
for horse-strength.

Mamá never married,
so I'm known as una bastarda
to those who feel free to scream.

Ilegítima almost sounds worse.
It's the church term, one that makes me seem
pointless, useless, lacking the validity of girls
whose fathers
accept them.

A single surname is the clue
that lets anyone,
even strangers,
understand the profound shame
of my illegitimacy.

People who like to be polite call me
una niña natural.
Abuela says that natural girls
are wild wonders,
like wind or the cool pool
of air
behind
a waterfall,
but mi abuelita
is one of only a few
people on earth
generous enough
to accept me as I am: Rima Marín,
a waif with a solitary surname
that means I have
only one parent.

I AM A LIVING, BREATHING SECRET

Natural children aren't supposed to exist.
Our names don't appear on family trees,
our framed photos never rest affectionately
beside a father's armchair, and when priests
write about us in official documents,
they follow the single surname of a mother
with the letters *SOA*,
meaning sin otro apellido,
so that anyone reading
will understand clearly
that without two last names
we have no legal right to money
for school uniforms, books, paper, pencils,
shelter,
or food.

Society expects natural children
to help everyone else
pretend
that we
are invisible.

HOME

Palm-bark walls, palm-thatched roof,
knotted hammocks, a rough, homemade table,
knobby chairs, and an outdoor kitchen
covered by flowering vines.

We have an outhouse, a makeshift shower,
a well, water jars, a laundry tub, a clothesline,
a chicken coop, fruit trees, and scattered patches
of corn, beans, yuca, and bananas, with plenty
of wild pasture for our horses.

Indoors, my world is a lacemaking workshop
of needles, thimbles, embroidery hoops,
crochet hooks, and flowing lengths
of delicate thread.

Outdoors, beyond the pastures, there is Abuela's
blacksmith shop, where rich men bring stallions
so that a famous female war veteran
with a reputation for healing skills
can tend the feet of champions,
swift steeds that win races
attended by foreign movie stars
and wealthy dignitaries
like my father.

The only problem
with our so-called home
is that it does not
belong to us.

We are squatters
on my father's land.

If he grows angry,
he can evict us,
leaving us
homeless
and hopeless.

WHEN IT RAINS ALL NIGHT

Our thatched roof leaks sun-heated
lizards and wasps.

Open spaces between loops of lace
offer clarity, the promise of blue
storm-cleansed air.

Dreams drift like starlight as my mind
floats restlessly toward tomorrow,
a place made of questions that can never
find answers.

Did Mamá ever love my father, or was he just
the source of wishes?
Did he pretend he would
marry her, and was the trick accepted
simply because she wanted to believe
his spidery web
of carefully crafted
lacelike
lies?

LA MAMBISA VOTING CLUB

Abuela founded her bold organization
long ago, after years as a nurse during the wars
for independence from Spain, in ferocious battles
that taught her how to race like a centaur
and live in the jungle, hiding while fighting
by healing
armed warriors
and their horses.

Most women's suffrage clubs consist only of ladies
who wear fancy gowns and diamond bracelets—
wives whose daughters have elaborate names
that are long enough to stretch and branch
like family trees, listing every twist and turn
of elegant
ancestry.

Not las mambisas.
Abuela is old, but she still gallops
like a supernatural being, along with
all the other women veterans who ride
as easily as they walk.

FEAR IS LIKE A SHADOW

Are las mambisas
fear-free?
No.
Abuela assures me that doubts
often swept into her mind on the battlefield
as she leaned over wounded soldiers,
striving to keep them alive
even when they were already losing
that final, precious breath.

Life and death,
so much responsibility!
Fear is like a shadow, always present
but sometimes hidden.

Abuela refuses to make lace.
Instead, she works as a farrier,
shaping sturdy horseshoes
from ferociously heated metal.
She says the sound of pounding tools
soothes her and helps her feel strong
like a tree in the forest, capable of sheltering
others.

LACEMAKERS

Whenever we are not riding or attending
Mambisa Voting Club meetings,
Mamá and I work side by side, our fingers
moving swiftly as we create lacy garments
for weddings, baptisms, First Communions,
and masquerade balls.

Our hands might look magical, but they ache
by the end of the day, all those loops and leaps
of sore fingers gradually transforming thread
into misty wisps,
like strands
of drifting fog.

Needle lace, bobbin lace, crocheted, knotted,
cutwork, and my favorite: filet lace, which I make
by embroidering pictures of flowers and birds
onto a fragile net that makes me think
of fishermen who work outdoors all day,
surrounded by nature's strength.

The brilliant, multicolored figures
that I stitch onto black or white filet lace
seem to float in midair, because from a distance
the dark or light net can only be seen

by someone who knows
it is there.

If only I could vanish
into the landscapes I create
as I embroider fanciful winged girls
and mermaids
with so many ways
to escape.

EXCLUDED

The hardest part of finishing
an intricate lace-edged bedspread or pillowcase
is delivering it to my half-sister's hostile mother.

My father's wife sends us work only to remind us
who we are: poor neighbors,
not
real
relatives.

She is, after all, the chosen one
who is married to the rich landowner.

Every time I see her legitimate daughter
I feel like I am the only sister
who has been sliced
in half.

INCLUDED

The educated ladies of fancy suffrage clubs
are making plans for a Women's Congress
in La Habana, where they will practice voting
by holding their own elections
about easy issues like kindness to animals
and difficult ones like equality
for natural children.

This will be the first time anyone has ever
openly discussed the illegitimate sons
and daughters
of indifferent fathers.

Caring for animals will be a swiftly accepted
charitable cause, but helping natural children
won't be easy to discuss, because so many of us
are the secret offspring
of those wealthy women's
roaming husbands.

They don't want us to receive surnames
or money for school, or the right to inherit
our fair portions
of fortunes.

So when las mambisas receive an invitation

to attend the Women's Congress, Abuela is thrilled,
but Mamá remains suspicious, convinced
that we will merely be a spectacle,
like an exhibit in a glass case
designed for staring.

Brown.
Poor.
Brave.
Specimens on display to satisfy the curiosity
of heiresses who drape their pale shoulders
in lacy shawls
        that we
            created
           with our own
        brave
      hands.

WHAT I'VE LEARNED
FROM LAS MAMBISAS

Strength of character is just as powerful
as muscles.

Hope soars like a spirited horse,
crossing fences and streams.

Confidence flutters and flies far away,
then returns, just as loyal
as a homing pigeon.

The mind of a horsewoman
loves stillness and patience
until wind lifts a leaf
releasing
fierce speed.

Courage.
Kindness.
Breathe.
Daydream.
Gallop.
Leap.

TRANSPORTED

The city of La Habana is only a one-hour walk away,
but we ride our horses, the same ones that carry us
at los rodeos, las cabalgatas, and las caballadas,
all the celebrations of horsewomanship
on festive holidays.

With long skirts flowing, we sit astride
like men, instead of sidesaddle
because we need
to center our balance
in case shouts, bells, or horns
startle our mounts.

By the time we arrive
at El Teatro Nacional
I am sweaty and nervous,
reluctant to be surrounded
by elegant ladies and their legitimate
daughters, who despise me simply for being
natural.

As a source of courage
I sing to myself quietly,
just as Abuela taught me,
listing all the ancestors whose lives
were so challenging.

Taíno families thrived on this island
long before the drastic European invasion,
Canary Islanders, Sevillanos, and Basques from Spain,
who brought Yorubas from Nigeria,
Berbers from Algeria,
and Cantonese from China,
all the people who joined
either willingly or forcibly
to create my unwritten
family tree.

Unfortunately, my anxiety is just as powerful
as the memory of those ancestors, so that I feel
as if my mind
is at war,
the breath
in both lungs
held captive
by tension.

If I don't resume
normal breathing soon,
will I faint?

Luckily, that first glimpse
of the astounding teatro
saves me, each gasp
of astonishment

at the beauty
of the building
filling my body
with inhaled
amazement.

ENCHANTED REALITY

Legends say El Teatro was built by a pirate
who became a fisherman, then constructed
a fish market, and finally decided
to try acting.

Stone statues of angels and heroes
perch all over the roof and walls
so that the sight of carved wings
inspires wild dreams of flight
on the theater's stage
and beyond.

Operas, tragedies, comedies, ballet,
every form of entertainment
has been performed on the same platform
that now holds an enormous flag
behind a row of tightly packed chairs
for the organizers of the First National
Women's Congress of Cuba.

Pilar Morlón de Menéndez.
Dulce María Borrero de Luján.
Antonia Prieto de Calvo.
Ofelia Domínguez Navarro.

Every one of these fancy ladies has two surnames.

That's why they invited me, isn't it—as an example
of natural childhood,
a specimen
to be studied?

In this auditorium designed for the leaps
and twirls of theatrical enchantment,
the solemn congress is joyfully introduced
as a first step toward gaining voting rights
for women, as well as establishing educational
and job training programs and helping puppies,
kittens, and the children
of the poor.

Within this clearly stated framework
of lofty goals, opinions vary.
Pilar—who is seated beside Señor Zayas,
el Presidente de la República de Cuba—speaks
eloquently of patience and the need
for gradual progress toward equality.

Dulce María is a poet who believes women
are too isolated at home and should receive
the creative inspiration of art classes.

Antonia proposes a program for introducing

sex education in schools, but even before
she finishes speaking, the shocked audience
churns like a hurricane, women in swirling skirts
hooting ugly names.

Finally, there is the bold voice of Ofelia,
a lawyer who argues passionately on behalf
of children like me, as if my ordinary life
has been touched
by magic.

Natural daughters and sons, Ofelia proclaims—
bellowing to drown out the dull arguments
of her opponents—are innocent victims
who deserve to share their fathers' surnames,
property, money, and that most enchanted
of all realities: respect.

I FEEL LIKE A ZOO CREATURE

I barely listen to the rest of the speakers.
Even a heated discussion
of the horrifying Adultery Law
fails to catch more than a sliver
of my attention.

Everyone already knows that murder is legal
whenever a man catches his wife
or daughter
with a lover.

A husband or father
can legally murder
the lover, too.

There will be no punishment.
Heat of the moment, emotions, justifiable vengeance.
Words passed down from thousands of years
of ignorance . . .

But my mind has abandoned the Adultery Law
and is twirling like a dancer all around Ofelia's
heartfelt plea for the rights of natural children.

The Adultery Law does not affect me,
because I don't have a father in my life
who would care enough to kill my mother

or me
for defying
his wishes.

So I gaze around
at the disapproving faces of ladies
whose dresses are decorated with lace
that I recognize as my own creation.

They stare at my feet as if I wore four hoofs
instead of two
rough cowhide boots
proudly fashioned by Abuela.

One mambisa's courage and skill
is more valuable to me than a thousand
snobbish
heiresses.

DISAPPOINTMENT

Forty-three speakers.
Seven days.
We can't afford to stay that long
without working, so we refuse Ofelia's invitations
to champagne receptions and field trips to orphanages,
maternity hospitals, nursery schools, nutrition programs,
concerts, and art exhibits.

When we ride home at the end of that first
humiliating day,
I feel like a zoo creature
freed from its prison.

We return to the city only once, for the final vote,
where formal support for female suffrage is approved
along with plans to demand a welfare system
and an immediate end
to the horrifying
Adultery Law. . . .

But none of these decisions made by women
have any legal status, because only men
can make government policies,
so this is just practice, a way for ladies
to imagine equality.

The next subject that comes up for a vote

is equal rights for natural children.

Rich women shriek, privileged wives
stamp their feet, and representatives
of church clubs declare their outrage,
as if they've forgotten that Jesucristo
cared about the needs of all children
even those whose mothers
never married.

Doña Pilar finally manages to restore order
in the auditorium, simply by agreeing to delay
the decision about natural children
until the next Women's Congress.

With a sigh, Ofelia tells me that means
that at least two years will pass before
wealthy women acknowledge my right
to exist.

DISBELIEF

I feel furious because the church
encourages disrespect for unwed mothers
and natural babies, but I don't blame God
because he believes in mercy.

No, I only blame rich men
who try to dominate
everything,
even heaven.

LA NATURALEZA

Home means nature,
and nature is heat, humidity, green and blue,
a dance of leaves
in such an intensely sunlit sky
that glancing up feels like flight
                          and looking down
                                 gives me
                                 roots.

Music flows all around whenever I walk through town
where vendors sing and old folks play dominoes outdoors,
their laughter rising on feathers of excitement.

What will life be like when I'm grown?
I love to imagine that by the time I'm old
natural girls will be symbols
of hope.

CONSTELLATION

Alone with our horseback boldness
and our landscapes made of lace,
Abuela, Mamá, and I form a picture,
like one made of drifting stars
that point the way toward dreams
of flight—equality—every girl's
                            brave wings.

PART TWO

THE SCHOOL OF HOPE

1925

NO MORE SCHOOL

We can no longer afford uniforms and books,
not even with the Gota de Leche
school lunch program
paid for by generous
feministas.

So I work at lacemaking,
and Abuela is teaching me
the art of horseshoeing.

I love the heated forge
long tongs
heavy anvil
noisy hammer
and the shape of a hoof
made of hot
pliable iron.

Pound.
Clang.
Hiss of coals.
Clinchers.
Knife.
Rasp.
Nippers.
Testers.

So many tools to protect
the foot of a trusting horse
from sharp stones
and tender
bruises.

The most satisfying moment
in this elaborate process
is fitting the lucky shoe
onto a spirited stallion
while my voice
calms him
and my hands
drive nails
into the hard hoof wall
all the time being careful to avoid
harming the soft frog—a sensitive
triangle of unprotected flesh
at the center of the bottom
of his foot.

Soreness.
Lameness.
An abscess.
A crack.
I learn how to heal thrush, laminitis,
canker, seedy toe, tying up, and quitter,
but some diseases have no remedy—
navicular, for instance.

Once that little
floating, boat-shaped bone
inside the foot of a racehorse
becomes arthritic,
his galloping days
are over.

It's the same
with me.

There's no cure for fear and shame
inspired by the noisy voices of insolent boys.

Their presence is the only thing I detest
about Abuela's otherwise soothing
workshop.

SKILL

Mamá gave me my own mare
as soon as I was old enough
to ride without clinging
to a saddle horn.

Now I gallop while waving a flag,
my free hand just lightly holding
the black, flowing mane
of Ala, my buttermilk buckskin
with her sun-hued sides, dark tail,
and zebra-striped legs, a horse
as beautiful and as unusual
as the natural artwork
of light and shadows
at the edge of a forest.

Learning to train her
has made me almost as confident
as the older mambisas, unless men
and boys are nearby
smirking.

UNITY

When el club performs all together
I absorb the strength of female hopes,
wondering if this is how it will be
someday
when women
can finally
vote!

ALA

My mare is my wing,
her hoofs the feathers
as she rises
sun-bound
cloud-fueled
soaring high
over fences
and streams. . . .

When we leap
I escape.

The enemy I run away from
is my own thought-trapped self,
all these doubts born within me.

If only I could mount a horse of hope
day and night, airborne, free!

FEAR ROAMS ALONE

                    Separated
from any other experience
    apart
            isolated
                    exiled
like an island that has floated
                            away
                        remote
and oh so close
both at the same time
            terror
dwells within me
                and beyond
simultaneously
                    gnawing
            scraping
strangling
my helpless
mind.

SURROUNDED

The blacksmith shop is a magnet
for rough men and rude boys
who never stop muttering insults
that lead to scornful laughter.

They accept Abuela as a farrier
only because she's a heroic mambisa,
but I'm just a natural child
surrounded by bullies.

I imagine galloping far away from fear
so I can breathe deeply, dream freely.
Hope is a raft
carried on sky waves
as I fly over walls
all this calmness
imaginary.

When I open my eyes
the bullies are still there,
and all my fears
of humiliation
return.

So I conjure images
of girls riding, women voting,

all of us defying the limitations
imposed by insults that result in
insulting
laws.

Even when I'm surrounded
by men and boys who expect me to fail,
I try to remember that I belong
to a sisterhood
of endless
determination.

POLITICS

When I'm shaping horseshoes, I inhale deeply
and listen quietly, while gruff men grumble
about Gerardo Machado y Morales,
the new presidente, who was elected
because his slogan—Cuba for Cubans—
seems to assure everyone that he won't allow
the United States Marines
to keep invading our island
every time their government
disapproves of our independence.

No more colonization!
Peace, prosperity, and modern roads!
High prices for exported sugar!
Low prices for imported steel!
No second term as president, either!
Every promise Machado makes
is an exclamation, especially
when he vows to step down
at the end of four years.

But skeptical men say that Machado
often makes secret deals
with rich gangsters from New York and Boston,
foreigners who come here only for gambling and rum,
simply because alcohol is illegal in their own country.

The men complain that it's all because
North American women can vote.

They claim—falsely—that Prohibition laws
passed in the US right after suffragists finally won
their long struggle in 1920, five whole years ago,
at a time when Mamá, Abuela, and I
still thought of carrying chairs
to weary store clerks
as the most daring act
of defiance.

If only suffrage efforts
had already succeeded.

Why do we have to wait so long
between protests, congresses,
and other attempts to make sure
that eventually our votes
and our voices
will be heard?

IMAGINING TRIUMPH

If these men ever asked me,
I'd say that Machado es un bruto
and my own abuela would be
a much better choice
for president.

The wisdom of old women
is worth so much more
than the vanity
of dictators.

DIVIDED

When my half-sister, Violeta,
picks up her new lace mantilla,
she scours me with an intensely curious gaze.

Glancing around at our palm-thatched house,
she must think of the rustic furniture
as primitive.

She is cool and pale
while I am warm brown,
but color is not the real barrier that separates us.
Legitimacy makes the difference.
She is accepted and lives with our father
whose wealth fills her life
with education.

If I am natural
what is she?

I strive to imagine that someday,
somehow, we might grow to understand
each other—at least well enough to be equals
if not
friends.

WHEN WORDS
BECOME MIRRORS

At the blacksmith shop, my half-brothers
tend to ignore me, but their friends
call me sinvergüenza, amazona, fea.

I know I'm not shameless or a muscular
female warrior, but am I ugly?
What do boys see when they look at me?
A shadow of my cigar-smoking abuela,
who places a ferocious scorpion under her hat
each time she feels the need
to relieve swelling?
She says the painful sting injects venom
that heals arthritis, but I'm afraid she's just
superstitious, her belief in curanderismo
left over from the past century.

If only I could stride like Violeta,
so snobbish and proud that no boy
would dare to insult her, for fear
of her father's—our father's—temper
and vengeance.

I DREAM OF BEING LEGITIMATE

My father would love me,
society could accept me,
strangers might even admire
my short, simple first name
if it were followed
by two surnames
instead of
          one.

FRIGHT IS A DISEASE
THAT CAN BE HEALED

Nightmares.
Breathlessness.
PANIC!

Each time one of the bullying boys
treats me like I'm a beast
instead of a person,
Abuela cures my attack of susto
by brushing me with a broom
of herbs, followed by a cleansing
with the smooth
white oval
of an egg,
then a freshly brewed tea
of soothing manzanilla
and bright cinnamon.

Each sip
tastes like freedom
from fear.

Everyone knows that susto
is a soul-flight illness
that can only be healed
in old-fashioned ways.

Even Mamá, with her firm belief
in modern medicine, can't help agreeing
that most male doctors don't understand
a teenage girl's uniquely
overpowering
anxiety.

Curing susto is a task
for fearless
old women.

THE NAME CURE

Abuela advises me to choose a nickname
for my frightened self: Rima Temor
for these times when I seem to be
nothing but a wisp
of fright.

Then she helps me choose another name
for my brave days: Rima Valor,
a sturdy girl made
of courage.

Surviving susto depends on knowing
which nickname to use when I talk
to myself
silently.

So inside my mind
I try to convince timid Rima Temor
that she must listen to the strong, valiant voice
of bold
Rima Valor.

MY QUIET TOWN

Guanabacoa is mostly peaceful.
Only the blacksmith shop gives me susto,
so I decide to give up the farrier work
and return to the creation of lace,
a way of making a living
that is silent and safe,
alone
with my mother
indoors.

The sense of loss
is a lot like feeling
haunted.

THE HISTORY OF
A QUIET TOWN

Guanabacoa is known as el pueblo de los indios,
even though four centuries have passed since Spain
forced our Taíno ancestors into the captivity
of soul-crushing
labor camps.

The churches are old and beautiful,
but their cemeteries contain more unmarked
indio graves
than any imagination of horrors can hold,
so we call our own great-great-grandparents
trembly ghosts
even though
we know
they are really
just the powerful spirits
of survival.

FRACTIONS

In church, my half-sister shuns me, perhaps
because her mother sits next to the man
who is also my
father.

Why did Mamá ever love him,
when it must have been so clear
that he would choose someone wealthy
and pale
to marry?

Once or twice each year
he glances at me, his gaze divided
between
fine rootlets
of curiosity
and a vast forest
of indifference.

If only I could vote to make laws
that would treat me as a whole person
instead of my father's fractured
mistake.

BEAUTIFICATION

I can't alter my frightened face, startled eyes,
or shadowy moods, but I can embroider lace,
a shawl of soaring horses, hoofs rising high
above any trace of shame
or fear.

When I drape the winged cloth
over my wide shoulders
and dark, flowing hair,
I feel ready
for anything,
even church.

Every time I ride Ala, I feel God's
love of freedom instead of society's
belief in harsh rules.

SERMONS

Today, natural children are the theme.
Evil, abysmal, despised, these are the words
used to describe us.

Silently, inside my mind, I invent a sermon
preached by angels instead of priests.
Gentle.
Resilient.
Wise.
If those are heaven's
generous words, imagine
what Dios might say.

Surely God sees no difference
between children who boast two surnames
and those of us who must learn to be satisfied
with fractions.

A GRAND GESTURE?

One Sunday after Mass,
Violeta appears in our doorway at dinnertime,
holding the most beautiful pair of riding boots
I have ever seen.

Sturdy but soft, the same sun-touched hue
as Ala's buttermilk buckskin flanks.

Un regalito, my half-sister announces.
But how can I accept the gift she describes
as little?

Mamá makes an effort to smile, but Abuela
merely shrugs as I take the boots, cradling them
like cuddly puppies.

Violeta stays and shares our simple meal
of white rice, black beans, and fried plátanos.

Instead of gracias, I tell her I'll wear the boots
at las caballadas, all the races, horseback ballets,
and festive holiday parades.

That's why I'm here, Violeta explains.
I want to join your voting club

and ride with las mambisas
at every performance.

So that's it, the boots are just payment
for a favor, not a gift, and certainly not small.
I'll be expected to teach this pampered princesa
how to gallop alongside all the old female patriots
who are so deeply revered
by the island's entire population.

Can Violeta balance without a saddle,
steer her mount without a bridle,
endure exhaustion, sore muscles,
biting flies, mud, dust?

Will she groom her own horse
or expect to bring servants?

Does my wealthy half-sister possess
even one tiny fraction of our club's
stubborn courage?

MINIATURE WORLDS

Details are the barely visible keys
to every important decision,
so I study my sister,
her sleek hair, delicate shoes, elegant clothes,
even the fragile glass buttons on her silky blouse,
each one a dazzling miniature work of art,
moon-hued and smooth
with enchanting bursts of color,
lavender petals and green
heart-shaped leaves
of tiny violets
that grow
and glow
from within
each sphere.

How did a glassblower create such magic
out of nothing but minerals, flames, and his own
breath?

If my name were ever transformed
into something as useful as a button,
it would have to be a tiny booklet.

Rima.
Rhyme.

Where would all the musical syllables fit?

By the time I notice that Mamá and Abuela
are both waiting for me to tell Violeta
whether she can ride with us, I've already
pictured an old glassblower, skinny and stooped,
frowning with concentration as he creates
huge buttons filled with flowers
and poems.

If only Mamá had named me after a blossom
with a lovely scent, instead of a verse, something
as simple as words.

I decide to tell Violeta she can ride in la cabalgata
de los tres reyes magos, but I warn her that she'll need
plenty of grueling practice, and we'll dance slowly,
because it's just a January 6 parade,
not a rodeo
or a race.

AT FIRST

We are strangers.
How can we ride together
when we don't respect each other?

I can't change my sister, so I'll have to alter
my own way of thinking, try to force
my imagination
to reach beyond
the narrow
limits
of history.

If we are ever going to succeed
in gaining suffrage for women
then certainly we'll need
to see all females
as equals.

At first resentment refuses to leave me,
but gradually, one practice session
after another
results in the change
I crave, as I rely on my horse
for guidance, because if Ala is happy
riding beside Violeta's mount, then I
can relax too,

gliding
at the canter
as if I can
fly.

HOOFBEATS

We practice together, Violeta and I,
as we ride to the beach, both of us
four-legged, swift, and so exhilarated
that we soon forget
all our differences.

I'm astonished by her skill.
Clearly, I underestimated my sister.

Light and dark, mi hermana y yo,
we gallop beside dolphins and flying fish. . . .

Her night-black stallion
and my sun-touched mare
form a herd of drumming heartbeats,
my brown skin and night-sky eyes
her pale face with blue-wave eyes—
dark and light
both
smiling.

THE SECOND
WOMEN'S CONGRESS

Violeta sits beside me
her back rigid with nervousness
or pride.

This time, there are seventy-one organizations
officially registered, forty more than before.
Unfortunately, Mamá says many are just phantoms
created at the last minute, a trick by priests and other
conservatives to gain votes opposing any proposal
that might grant mercy
for natural children.

I'm sure Jesucristo would agree with me:
church and God do not always share
the same
goals.

The first speeches are made in favor
of social welfare causes, such as the Red Cross,
Band of Mercy, and other charities for the humane
treatment of poor people and animals,
as well as public health, music, art. . . .

Later, talks turn toward the Adultery Law and voting,
the only two subjects where all delegates agree
completely that yes, women deserve suffrage,

and no, angry husbands should not
be allowed to kill wives
or daughters.

After several days of less controversial subjects,
the most difficult debate is finally faced,
and once again Ofelia becomes my hero
as she advocates vehemently
passionately
powerfully
for the rights
of natural children.

Just as before, conservatives shout her down,
condemn her as immoral, accuse her of protecting
bastards, and speculate on the origin
of her opinions, wondering if she is secretly
the mother of an illegitimate baby.

Rage and hatred storm through the hall
where women argue, stamping hard heels
and slamming heavy chairs
against the floor
so that not even a modest
compromise
can be reached.

No surname, no money, no shelter.
The natural children of indifferent fathers

are still not entitled to any benefits at all,
not even a symbolic statement of respect.

Fuming like dragons, Ofelia and eight other delegates
storm out of the auditorium in protest,
so Abuela, Mamá, and I stand up and follow them
while my half-sister stays in her seat, avoiding
my wounded
gaze.

AFTERMATH

Violeta and I barely speak
as we pirouette on sidesaddles,
practicing our most challenging
horseback ballet.

If she wants to be friends,
she'll have to explain why
I should trust anyone
who thinks I'm inferior
and should remain invisible.

Insults from boys are bad enough.
The disdain of my own half-sister
feels like a betrayal.

If our situations were reversed,
wouldn't I accept Violeta
as my equal?

TURMOIL

When I finally forgive my sister just enough
to listen without speaking, she tells me she stayed
in the auditorium only to see what would happen.

Machado spoke, promising that he
would grant the vote to women.

Then, after the meetings ended, he sent thugs to arrest
students, workers, labor leaders, and anyone else
who dares to speak out against his wave of censorship
and repression.

Now women will have to decide whether
to support him, in exchange for suffrage.

Ofelia, as it turns out, is his most daring opponent.
Instead of speaking to newspapers or radio stations,
she marches directly to the house of Machado's mother
and convinces the old woman to scold her tyrannical son.
But even that small female triumph is not enough
to stop
the violence.

THE SERENITY OF HORSES

With the entire country in an uproar,
I find refuge by grooming Ala, brushing dust
from her coat, cleaning her hoofs,
stroking her face, inhaling
the breath of a creature
that has no need
for words,
just touch.

Nothing has ever calmed me as thoroughly
as this slow companionship
the shadows and light
heavy head and gentle eyes
of a massive creature
who allows a puny human
to share
restfulness.

PART THREE

HEROES, HURRICANES, AND HEARTBREAK

1926–1927

RITUALS

Knowing what to expect comforted me on Christmas,
when we walked all over town, admiring each family's
nacimiento, quaint arrangements of ceramic shepherds,
livestock, and the Holy Family, all displayed
near open windows
so that we could look in,
just as our neighbors
were peering into our house
to see rustic wooden figurines
surrounded by folds
of exquisite lace.

At midnight we attended a candlelight Mass,
then came home and ate slices of fruit with crunchy nuts.

On New Year's Eve we mopped our earthen floor
and tossed the dirty water outside, to rid our lives
of last year's discouragement.

Twelve grapes, twelve wishes—I swallowed as quickly
as I could, to prepare myself for a dozen months of luck.
Now, on New Year's Day, we work hard at making lace
and horseshoes,
reminding ourselves
that the way we behave

during each of the next twelve days
will predict our fortunes
for the entire
year.

THREE KINGS' DAY

On January 6,
la cabalgata de los tres reyes magos
is a spectacular tradition, our horses
elaborately decorated as we dance
behind three costumed men
who represent the wise kings.

Violeta and I toss candy and small toys
to children who follow us, shouting
"¡las mambisas!"
as if they really believe
we are white-haired warriors
like Abuela.

I've heard that in North America,
gifts are given on Christmas morning
under a decorated tree, but I can't imagine
a better time and place for celebration
than in this parade
of survivors.

HEROISM

The next morning, on our quiet patio,
Abuela tells me the story of Rosa la Bayamesa
a nurse who hid in wilderness caves for decades,
healing the sick and wounded soldiers
of both sides, during all three wars
for freedom from Spain
and liberation from slavery.

Abuela continues this history lesson
with the story of Magdalena Peñarredonda y Doley,
who freed a captive rebel when she was only five,
and María Hidalgo Santa, a flag bearer who led charges
into battle, and Ana Betancourt, who spoke boldly
at the 1869 Constitutional Congress, demanding
female equality.

Later, during the early days of voting clubs,
there were protests against the 1901 Constitution,
because it continued to ignore women's rights.

In 1909, impoverished laundresses
from the Railroad Washing and Ironing Guild
marched for equal pay, but police attacked
the protesters, then blamed them
for the violence, arresting

their brave leader,
Justa Martínez.

By the time Abuela falls silent,
I'm eager to speak up on behalf
of natural children, the most urgent cause
from my point of view—along with suffrage,
of course, because until women gain
the right to vote
my voice
will not
be heard.

ACTIVISM

Together with Violeta and all the heroic old women
of our Voting Club, I ride to the city to listen as Ofelia
and other feministas
outline plans
for job training programs.

Unlike my half-sister, I don't have a rigid father
who will try to marry me off to a rich man or a mother
who is so busy organizing country club luncheons
that she doesn't even notice that the French governess
happens to be a suffragist who encourages Violeta
to attend rebellious rallies.

Maybe I could ask Ofelia for a chance to choose
a career goal, but so far the job training programs
are limited to pharmacist, typesetter, and artist.

There is nothing for lacemakers or farriers.
Do I have the courage to try a completely
new skill?

UNCERTAINTY

As soon as I compare my poverty
to my half-sister's astounding wealth,
I end up feeling confused.

In some ways, I might be more free
to choose the path of my future,
even though she has an education,
countless luxuries, and the prospect
of marrying someone
who will see her
as worthy of respect.

So what can I do to overcome fear
and make my vision
clear?

HARD AND SOFT

My heart

is   like

a   horse

hoof   that

strikes   a bruise   sparks

the   center

fragile   tender

STRUGGLING TO UNDERSTAND MYSELF

At
the peak
of a treetop
of questions
about courage
I'm left with only
hope, which like lace
is both sensitive and strong
my
————two————
deeply
rooted
hidden
natures.

FIFTEEN

Violeta's quince will be celebrated
by adults, government officials, even foreign
movie stars and famous singers, everyone flocking
to her father's mansion like hummingbirds
to a golden
trumpet flower.

Or should I say *our* father's mansion?
But natural daughters never receive
parties
presents
attention
guests.

There will be no festivity for me
when I turn fifteen; it will just be
one more day of ordinary
confusion.

WORK

I'm making the white lace for my half-sister's elaborate
party dress, which resembles a wedding gown.
She wants fifteen miniature angels on winged horses
all in the space of a bodice and sleeves.
The rest of the long flowing garment
will be designed and stitched overseas, in France.
Her shoes will come from Italy, her diamond tiara
from Tiffany's in New York, and the button closure
for her absurdly warm silver fox fur cape
will be made by the same local glassblower
who knows how to infuse moon-smooth
surfaces
with the breath
of dreamlike
visions.

PICTURE BUTTONS

Violeta treats me like a servant.
She sends me to pick up the circle of glossy magic
that will hold her fur wrap in place until she's ready
to open it and reveal the details of my lacy tribute
to las mambisas.

The glass studio is even hotter and more mysterious
than Abuela's farrier shop, with fires glowing,
sand glinting, minerals shimmering,
and the agate eyes of the glass artist
radiating curiosity.

I expected a sullen old man, but the glassblower
is young, handsome, friendly,
so eager to show me his work
while asking about lace, horseshoes,
rodeos, and la cabalgata de los tres reyes magos,
where he saw me riding along with Abuela
and so many other
national heroes.

To my surprise, I enjoy at least thirty seconds
of calm before the usual waves of boy-fear
seize me.

Ordinarily, whenever we need buttons

for clothes, we carve disks of wood, bone,
horn, or the smooth, ivory-like seeds
of tagua palm trees.

I would make buttons from seashells, too,
if Abuela didn't keep warning me that bringing
any remnant of the ocean into our home
is an invitation to floodwaters
during the storm surge
of a hurricane.

Glass buttons have always been a luxury
far out of reach, just like imported jewelry
and bottles of manufactured perfume.

I've never owned anything that sparkled
like starlight, so now, when the artisan
presents me with a glittering gift,
I can hardly believe
it's real.

Sun-hued, the button
            is a portrait of Ala,
            her eyes dark
                neck arched
                and on her back

a longhaired beauty:
me.

Ordinarily, I would remain terrified by the voice,
shoulders, hands, and height of this strange boy,
but somehow his portrayal of me on horseback
eases my anxiety to such a degree that I smile.

You should be able to vote, he says with conviction,
and you should also keep galloping instead of settling
into the seat of any omnibus or automobile.
Las mambisas, he observes, bring the best
of both centuries
together.

Old and new, he adds, like glass art
in a time when most people just want buttons
and hat pins made in a factory, thousands
of identical duplicates, all crafted
without imagination
or passion.

As soon as he utters that word
I flee with Violeta's huge button
and my more delicate gift
both clutched tightly

in my sweaty fists
as my heart drums
and my tumbling mind
shudders at the sound
of those syllables: pasión.

EXCITEMENT

Away from the reach of his gaze
fear changes to jittery bliss.

Never before have I freely imagined
myself in the arms of un novio,
a boyfriend, maybe even
someday
a husband. . . .

Galloping is always just like this,
lightning-flash flames of joy,
a blaze!

AFTER EXCITEMENT

Fantasies are glamorous, but real life
does not always rhyme.

What if that artisan made a flattering picture
on a button
just to mock me?

I open my fists.
The design of a girl on horseback
is alive with imaginative details,
while the button for Violeta
merely shows her wealth—white glass
clasped within a thick circle
of gold.

I would rather possess
a treasury of imaginación
than any amount
of shiny metal.

EYES

Unable to resist, I turn back to the studio
and ask the boy how he created a horse and rider
who seem to be magically encased
inside a miniature
world
of sunshine.

"Intaglio" is his answer, a design etched
with tiny tools that sink every line
deep below the silky surface, creating
unimaginably fine details that are combined
with paint, colors, light. . . .

While he demonstrates
on a disk of clear glass, I study his face.
Rich brown like his skin, the iris of each eye
speckled, streaked with light, an agate
that contains sun and night
flesh and stone.

Exchanging gazes, we glimpse
each other's shyness.

RELIEF

It's a scene that is mine now
this insight:
boys can be timid too.
I have nothing to fear
in the presence
of respect.

ONE BUTTON IS ENOUGH TO CHANGE MY DAYDREAMS

None of my clothes are worthy of such a fine ornament,
so I keep it hidden in the pocket of a shabby skirt
where I can reach down and touch the cool surface,
rolling it between my fingers like a worry stone
or a rosary.

This is real, Ala might say if she could speak.
There truly is one unique boy
who sees me
as more
than una bastarda.

ALTERED

All my life, I've watched Mamá rip out old seams
and replace them with new, making garments
wider or narrower to fit pregnant women
or those who are already busy mothers,
slim and hungry because they devote
every scrap of food and energy to their children.

Suddenly, I feel like one of those torn threads
in an old seam with ragged edges and no way
to avoid the substitution of something
beyond my control, a sharp needle,
expert stitches, the shape of my future
already changing. . . .

Yesterday I was afraid of all boys, but now
I'm eager to admit that the young glassblower
intrigues me, his eyes just as appealing
as the gift he gave me, this sunny circle,
a vision that I hold
in my mind.

TWO BIRTHDAYS

Seen from a distance, the mansion erupts
with fireworks and noise, a booming orchestra
to celebrate Violeta's vibrant future.

A few days later, my own cumpleaños is just another
quiet evening at home, with nothing to make
the number fifteen
special.

If only I knew how to stop comparing my poverty
to my half-sister's riches.

It's our father's fault for rejecting me
and accepting her, so why am I the one who feels
guilty
and useless
just because she enjoyed
a lavish quince?

SERENADE

Moonlight, guitar music, and a boy's
familiar voice.

Estas son las mañanitas—birthday lyrics,
the song about little mornings . . .

Awake, I stand in our doorway, silently thrilled
to see the glass artist here, right here, strumming
and singing just the way all girls imagine
una serenata should be.

In daydreams, the singer is always polite enough
to vanish after his song, but in real life, he waits
for me to introduce him to Mamá and Abuela.

His name is Maceo, and he works with his father,
who makes all the stained-glass windows
for local churches.
He's been working since he was little,
but he's also in school, and he's traveled
to glass shops in Mexico. . . .

My mother disapproves, I can tell right away,
but Abuela seems willing to believe
that glass is a miraculous creation,
especially in churches, with panes

of crystalline color
outlined
by narrow
pathways
of metal.

By the time Maceo leaves, I feel certain
that my grandmother wants me to like him,
but Mamá is so cold that I wonder if she assumes
he could turn out to be just as devious
as my father.

SISTERHOOD

The next day, Violeta comes to visit, whispering
that she too has a novio, but if her Papá finds out
that she's kissed a boy, she'll be locked in her room
like a storybook princess.

She presents me with a birthday gift,
a whole set of blue glass buttons,
enough for the most elegant dress.

Each surface shows a white dove
carrying a green branch, offering
peace
paz
amistad
the friendship
of sisters.

I have no worthy clothing, so I drop the small treasures
into my pocket, along with the first one, both horse
and rider now surrounded
by glossy wings.

A SENSE OF PURPOSE

Girls are never supposed to pursue boys,
so I stay where I am, trapped in a routine
of work,
daydreams,
galloping. . . .

Ala is my guide, a four-legged explorer
who leads me along trails far beyond
my own understanding.

Together, Violeta and I share so many
dizzying adventures that it's hard for me
to remember what days were like before,
when my only riding companions
were a mother and grandmother
who already knew all my secrets.

Now, my half-sister confides so many
scandalous details of her romance
that I don't want to admit I've never
even touched Maceo's hand.

Will he come back to serenade me again,
or was it just a yearly song, a simple
birthday gift?

I'm fifteen, plenty old enough to marry,
have babies, responsibilities, worries, debts . . .
but all I really want
is justice.

Imagine if I could earn enough money
for silk dresses with glass buttons,
but instead of wearing them to banquets,
I'd give them away to charity, to be worn
by the natural daughters of other stubborn
unfair fathers.

There is no room in my life for a novio,
not if I want to be a truly dedicated
feminista
like Ofelia.

LISTENING

Every time Ofelia speaks, we travel
to the city to hear her impassioned pleas.
She introduces us to essays written by
Mariblanca Sabas Alomá, who explains
that women do not want to be rich men's
enemies; we just want freedom
and equality, the same prizes sought
by poor men.

Everything makes so much sense
when I focus my attention on adults
who have already considered the need
for suffrage
from every angle.

Listening allows me to learn without repeating
foolish errors, because at every one of those meetings
there are always wealthy women who rant against
natural children, trying to convince everyone
that bastardas are to blame
for our own birth.

FURY

At one of Ofelia's meetings, we learn
that suffragists from the United States
have mocked us in the most shocking
and hurtful manner, treating us like inferiors
simply because our skin
is brown.

It happened at an international conference
in Panamá, where Carrie Chapman Catt,
director of the Women's Struggle for World Peace
and Friendship with South America,
said that we—all the feministas
of Latin America—do not deserve
to vote.

She described us as childlike,
irresponsible, immature.

Now Ofelia denounces those vicious words
as racism, leaving me with a grief that feels
as deep as the sorrow
after a death.

I thought we could count on support
from women who have already triumphed
in their struggle, but instead, all we receive

are insults
and the hollow promises
of Machado,
who never fulfilled
his vow to grant suffrage.

He no longer feels that he needs
the support of women.

All he wants is power, and that is a prize
he has already seized.

When I think of all the obstacles we face
both at home and abroad, every splinter
of sadness
is transformed
into rage.

RESISTANCE

Violeta keeps asking me to meet
her novio, and she continues
trying to send me to the glass shop
to fetch buttons, beads, vases,
glasses, candleholders, figurines,
trinkets, and sculptures
that she's commissioned,
but I don't need
her matchmaking skills.

I tell myself that all I want
is independence, even though
the memory of Maceo's eyes
meeting mine
still feels
undeniably
clear
and
radiant.

DEVASTATION

In October 1926, the fury of a hurricane
joins my own confused rage, destroying
entire neighborhoods
throughout La Habana
and beyond.

The wind
is a hunger
that swallows
houses, fields,
hopes.

¡Ciclón!
¡Peligro!
¡Cuidado!
Bellowed warnings from Mamá and Abuela mean little
when we have no place to hide, no refuge, no shelter,
no strong stone walls like Violeta's.

So we turn our horses loose, slap their flanks,
and tell them to run, find safety, escape. . . .

Expecting to die, I barely believe my eyes
when I see Maceo
rushing toward me through the barrage
of airborne objects—palm fronds, oxcarts,

and chicken coops—
all swirling through torrents
of rain
that roar
like monsters.

He guides us uphill,
dodging flash floods
and whirlpools
until we reach
the sturdy
warehouse
behind
his family's
glass shop.

Walls of mampostería, the sturdy
broken-stone form of adobe
that is held together with a mortar
of clay, bricks, and coral,
any block of any shape
wedged together
like fragments
of a puzzle.

Within the warehouse, we'll be safe.
Inside Maceo's world of stone and glass
wind and water won't reach me.

My only vulnerability will be
this fragile window of emotion
called attraction.

SAFETY

In the warehouse
we're surrounded by people,
Maceo's entire family—parents, sisters,
brothers, uncles, aunts, cousins, grandparents,
and neighbors.

Fearful, I cringe, avoiding noisy boys
and leering men, ominous strangers . . .
until Maceo takes my arm and leads me from one
marvel to another, showing me all the intricate
creations made by his ancestors: stained glass,
blown glass, and statues.

LOSS

Will any of our own crafts survive
the storm, or has wind already claimed
horseshoes tangled in nets of lace?

What about Ala and our other horses?
Why didn't we bring them with us
into this magnificent fortress of stone?

For now there does not seem to be a future,
just this vigil, the slow process of waiting
like an internal hurricane, spinning
and twisting
my thoughts.

VIGIL

Waiting for the end of a hurricane
is a strange form of lost-in-time torment.

I'm usually soothed by any chance to learn
how to make things with my own hands,
but in a frantic crowd of panicked refugees,
no blowpipe or burner can calm me.
Molds, paddles, shears, grinding wheels,
engraving lathes, tweezers, hooks—the glass shop
contains even more implements than a farrier's
elaborate collection of useful tools, and these furnaces
are just as dangerous, with burns and explosions
a constant threat, and if I add to that all the fumes,
poisons, and silica dust that can damage Maceo's lungs,
I begin to wish he would choose
some other
passion.

He shows me the slow process
of controlled cooling called annealing,
with small bubbles
referred to as seeds
and larger crystalline lumps known as stones,
the surface of glass transformed into patterns
I'd never imagined—opalescent, iridescent,

even layered,
one color above another
like water
in a whirlpool.

Maceo's father demonstrates how he etches,
polishes, or paints some of the objects,
resulting in works of art that reflect or refract
like stars in a distant galaxy.

Butterflies and birds appear to fly
inside spheres of glass, while other creatures
perch on top, frogs and turtles looking restful.

By the time the storm ends three days later,
I already know that our thatched house
probably rose into turbulent sky
and vanished, but what about the horses?
How will I ever
find Ala?

I tell myself I had no choice,
but that doesn't chase my guilt away.
I turned her loose without imagining
that Maceo would have welcomed her

here, into this refuge
made of colors
and light.

Even if she'd smashed all the glass
with her hoofs, he would have stroked Ala
to calm her, simply because he knows
how it feels
to be needed.

If only I had trusted him
as much as I trust
my horse.

Heartbreak can take so many forms.
I feel like my arteries and veins
are shrinking.

AFTER A STORM

The sky is finally calm enough to suggest safety.
I step outdoors and walk beside Mamá and Abuela,
determined to discover any remnants of our house.

Only a few scraps remain,
but the blacksmith shop has suffered
less damage, and all three horses are safe!

Ay, Ala, what would I do without you?
Our winged hopes would vanish,
my imagination reduced to two
human legs, instead of our shared
four, the miracle of blending
your speed with my mind
turning us into a centaur. . . .

How grateful I am that Violeta sheltered you
in her family's stable, and now she offers us
housing too, at least until we have a chance
to rebuild.

It will be a struggle,
but waiting for suffrage
has taught us patience.

Mamá refuses to enter

my half-sister's home,
so we sleep surrounded
by farrier tools,
wondering if it's true
that horseshoes
are lucky.

I understand my mother's reluctance
to accept charity from the family
that has tormented her, but now
I no longer think of Violeta
as unmerciful.

Would I be as generous
to her, if our roles were
reversed?

LEAP UP TOWARD LOVE

Throw your heart over the fence
and your horse will follow.
It's a saying las mambisas repeat so often
that sometimes I barely listen, but tonight
the brave words seem as true for relationships
as for riding.

If I toss my emotions high above a wall of fear
will my anxious mind follow?

Love
is a leap,
not a fall.

The next time I see Mateo, I'll thank him
for saving us from the hurricane, and then
I'll touch his hand to see how it feels
when reaching fingers
meet
in midair.

EARTHBOUND

Ala's breath is sweet with the scent
of wildflowers as she swivels her ears
to catch any sound from another storm.

Are we safe?
It's impossible to know.

Abuela says sometimes hurricanes strike
back-to-back, another rumbling in right over
the rubble of buildings tumbled by the last one.

We have no choice but to work
as if tomorrow
is not dangerous.

This time our house will be like the warehouse
with walls of broken stone that we can cement
using a mortar of mud, straw, and gravel, decorated
by inserting bits of coral, both the orange form
and the black.

VULNERABLE

Each day is unpredictable
hideous cyclones and nature's beauty
so closely intertwined that anything
seems possible.

When Maceo stops by to see how we are,
he stays to help build our new walls,
showing us how to design windows
with wooden shutters for protection
and crescent moon-shaped
stained-glass lunetas
for beauty.

I lose the courage to touch him, but within a few days
our new house looks like an aviary, the glass wings
of colorful birds stretching above each ordinary
square
of open air.

If only we were not squatters
building a home that can be toppled
by the real landowner at any moment.

BIRDS AND WORDS

At night I gaze up at slivers
of multicolored glass wings
illuminated
by the moon.

How will we live?
Abuela's arthritis grows worse
each day, and Mamá says she's tired of making lace.

When Ofelia visits, we ask for information
on job training programs sponsored by voting clubs.
My mother selects pharmacy school, hoping to help
my grandma find a cure that does not require
painful scorpion bites.

I choose typesetting.
Each row of letters
will be arranged
as thoughts
on the page
of a newspaper
or magazine.

Imagine how far
those thoughts

can reach
once the paper
begins
to travel!

ALPHABET

Rows, columns, determination,
a printshop filled with women.
Even the instructor is female!

How easily I breathe here
surrounded by letters, words, paragraphs,
punctuation, and the miraculous emergence
of pages.

Paper, ink, modern gadgets,
and the medieval weight of a printing press
as I turn a wheel, leaning to move it with all
my strength.

Vocabulary, pronunciation, translations,
I feel like I've already traveled the whole world,
moving across maps
of time
and place.

PART FOUR

ANGELS AND ASSASSINS

1927–1929

ALMOST FEARLESS

Working in a printshop feels
as courageous as any horse race.

Like the bright-winged bird-angels
in one of Maceo's stained-glass
lunetas, I soar back and forth
between imagination
and reality.

The alphabet seems like a family
I can depend on to help me express
any wish.

All I have to do is pretend I'm the writer
whose bold words appear on brave paper
as I organize
roll
print.

MOVABLE TYPE

The blocky three-dimensional letters
made of metal
are called
sorts.

I place *M* in a press, ink the surface, and use
my strength
to crank a wheel, leaving an impression
of paired mountain peaks on smooth paper.

Why *M*?
For Maceo!

Ofelia disapproves.
R, she insists, should be my first concern.
RIMA, followed by my solitary but proud surname.
Rima Marín—I must know myself before I seek
companionship, she instructs, and last of all
comes love, because it can only exist after I am free
of traditional
expectations.

TURNING THE WORLD
UPSIDE DOWN

I pick up each block-like sort
with my right hand, set it into a composing stick
held in the left, then arrange letters, words, verses
that look
inverted.

When poets start asking for me as their favorite
typesetter, I feel flattered but confused—why me?
Because of my name is the universal answer: Rima.
They think of me as a walking, living, breathing
rhyme!

Body, shank, point size, shoulder, nick, groove,
foot, set, width, flong, hot metal, Linotype, hellbox,
casting matrix, monotype, typograph, letterpress . . .

The words that describe various methods
make me dizzy with excitement and nervousness.

What if I make mistakes and destroy
some impoverished poet's dream?

STUDIOUS

Ay, how I love to learn!
Why did I ever let anyone stop me
from staying in school?

From now on, I know who I am.
Rima Marín, lifelong student
of life.

Poetry is a mystery.
Designing pages for a book,
I learn how to observe; I look
beyond the sounds of verse, deeply,
inside, where wild parts of me
understand the need to be
a bridge between a free
flowing river of simple words
and the poet's emotions, heard
as echoes, bell-like, pure, a plea.

WE NEED EQUAL PAY

Weekly wages!
I will never again underestimate
the freedom from worry that is granted
by a dependable salary.

Mamá earns money too,
but both of us soon realize
that we make much less than men
who do exactly the same kinds
of typesetting apprenticeship
and pharmacist's assistantship—
such highly skilled work.

What use were all those protests
when nothing has changed, no voting rights,
no equality for natural daughters, no end
to the horrifying Adultery Law?

Sometimes I still feel like a hardworking child,
one who receives weekly wages along with daily
discouragement.

A FEMINISTA APPRENTICESHIP

After completing my training, I work for a woman
who prints books written and illustrated by poets,
essayists, philosophers, and artists
who oppose all sorts of profitable trends,
choosing to resist oppression of the poor
by the rich.

Each page I typeset
helps me enjoy the liberty of words
as I join the peaceful resistance
against Machado's brutality.
He has rewritten the constitution,
extending his presidency
to a six-year term and banned
all political parties except his own.
In any future election, he will run
unopposed, and even now, anyone
who criticizes his tyranny
is fed to sharks
that lurk
in gloomy
waters.

Now I see why Machado never kept his promise
to grant women's suffrage—he knows he does not

need our support, because he never planned to let
ANYONE
male or female
vote
freely
ever again.

He has plunged this entire nation
into the dangerous chaos that fuels
any dictatorship.

All I can do is oppose him quietly,
relying on the strength of the alphabet,
as I arrange powerful thoughts
one
by
one,
contributing to page
after page
of truth.

WHISPERING

Complaining about a tyrant
is so perilous that when feministas meet
we speak in riddles, whispers, gestures,
rolling our eyes and waving our hands
to show that we still have a simmering
fire
of resistance.

How did an entire country allow one elected leader
to transform himself into a self-appointed king?

We speak in metaphors, ordinary conversations
converted into thunder, lightning, volatile,
explosive. . . .

The words we use to describe weather
are really descriptions of our own reactions
to a storm of injustice that has swept
all freedom away
as if the recent hurricane
reached into human hearts
with handcuffs.

REBELLIOUS RIDDLES

Even Ofelia speaks more carefully now,
communicating through unspoken
gestures and actions, bringing me
pamphlets, posters, and rhymes.

The poets whose work I print
write in ways that say so much
without appearing to convey
anything political.

Gardens in the poems are prisons.
Flowers in the verses
are revolutionaries.
Birdsongs
are guns.

SECRECY

how unusual
it feels to whisper horrors
that are all too true
while hiding their real meanings
in a forest of metaphors

THE STRENGTH OF A PAGE

each poem I print
is passed along quietly—
this paper-thin hope

LOVE IN A TIME OF FEAR

Abuela cares for all three horses,
grooming, feeding, and exercising Ala
when I'm too busy.

Violeta's visits seem normal,
her only topic of conversation
the looks, talents, and attentions
of her beloved novio.

We never meet him.
Sometimes I wonder if her boyfriend exists,
or is he merely hidden because her father—
our father—would not approve?

When I enter the glass shop to speak with Maceo,
I feel as if I'm spinning inside an alternate universe
where my anxieties turn to passion and one kiss
is enough to
change everything.
One kiss, this time real instead of imaginary.
One kiss, and then another, each one radiant
like stained glass or printed paper . . .

RESISTANCE

Gracias a Dios, Maceo is the rebel I hoped
he would be, just as outraged by Machado's
tyranny as I am, even though we rarely
dare to speak openly
about
details.

When we say los tiburones, we mean the sharks
that grow fatter each time an enemy of the dictator
is tossed off a boat, but in case anyone is listening,
we pretend we're speaking of a statue
commissioned by a yacht club.

I know I'll go to jail or be thrown into the sea
if I'm caught printing some of the poetry
that rejects metaphors and states its case
boldly.

I have to treat each private conversation
with the same care, unable to trust
even the thickest, most storm-resistant
broken stone wall.

POETRY IS GLORIOUS

Each volume is printed in such small numbers
that only those who really love freedom
will have a chance to read these verses of protest.

The beauty of handmade book covers
is my newest contribution, along with
this painstaking labor of typesetting,
followed by the risk of secretive
distribution.

Stamped leather, fine cardboard,
even sculpted wood can enclose pages.
I love to imagine a volume of rhymes
treasured between two sheets
of stained glass, as if readers
will always be careful enough
to trust the poems of strangers
to something so fragile
and powerful.

THE ART OF PROTEST

Press-molded, sheared, beveled, fire-polished,
table-polished, foiled . . .

Of all the techniques for making glass that resembles
natural gemstones, lampworking is my favorite.

Maceo reheats blown clear tubes of various colors,
then works them into enchanting designs.

I watch as he twists and twirls softened facets
into petals, leaves, and wings, bringing dreams
of mythical creatures into fantastic forests.

When he spins glass into fine threads,
we can weave the strands into fabric,
creating layers of glowing light
as if the cover of a book
were alive.

COLLABORATION

We kiss.
Embrace.
Share hope.

Then I crochet lacy edges
around natural leaves, while he encases
pearls and diamonds of light
within the curves of glass birds
and fish, turning symbols of freedom
and mercy
into figurines
that can be attached to books
as decorations.

Stars, meteors, moon, there is no prayer
or wish that cannot be made visible
once we rise and float
toward love.

WHEN POETS AND JOURNALISTS DISAPPEAR

we know
their bones are in the bellies
of sea beasts
but their dreams live on
in soft hopes and strong actions

INTERVIEW

Las mambisas meet for the first time in months
to speak, smile, ride, race, and sing about the need
for more voting clubs where women can organize
and plan.

Waiting.
Waiting.
Waiting for equal rights!
I look around at the faces,
wrinkled, wizened, sun-scorched,
every shade of brown, black, and white skin
is included in this group that formed so long ago,
some fighting with machetes, others by curing
the wounds of soldiers.

This time the battle is a mirror of patience,
our words like shadows slicing through time
as las mambisas agree to be interviewed
by reporters who ask the old warriors
if they will support Machado
in exchange for suffrage.

Abuela's response is straightforward
and fearless—no, she won't compromise
with a bully whose only skill is terror.

Voting requires at least two candidates,
not just one who imagines that he
can cling to power forever.
She'd rather wait
wait
wait
for justice.

NEVER RELENT

Maceo and I don't give up designing
beautiful covers for powerful books,
not even when his father warns him
to be cautious.

Imprisonment.
Torture.
Death.
All the threats of suffering
are the fuel that keeps a tyrant in power,
flames fed by fear consuming the future,
even before the present is past, but for now
we are alive and in love.

University students.
Doctors.
Professors.
The people who disappear
live on in our
protests.

NO MORE HYPOCRISY

When a poet vanishes
I don't know if my book was the cause.
All I did was print many copies of a fish designed
by Maceo, a symbol of Jesucristo's generosity,
but also an indirect statement against churches
that oppose
equality
and justice.

Real cristianos don't support
Machado
and his sharks.

The lost poet's words live on as I print more and more
copies of verses about caring for orphans, widows,
and natural babies instead of wealthy gangsters,
gamblers, and corrupt policemen.

ANOTHER FORM OF RESISTANCE

Mamá is always busy with her pharmacy
apprenticeship, but if we were still lacemakers,
we'd be in demand, because the new flapper fashions
require fringed skirts and intricate shawls.
Dresses are short.
Dances are bold.
Women grow confident.
Bobbed hair.
Painted lips.
Smoky eyes.
Slender cigars
and jazz, jazz, jazz!
Each time I see my half-sister, she's draped
in shimmering beaded sheaths, arms bare,
legs exposed, face sparkling under layers
of glittery makeup, short hair barely concealed
by tiny hats that resemble beehives or half-moons.

Violeta is so caught up in her whirlwind
of parties, rumbas, and rum that she forgets
to ride with las mambisas or join our whispered
conversations
with other feministas.

Her rebellion is against our father,
not the government.

If he had his way, she would be engaged
to a rich man, instead of her ordinary
working-class novio, a boy she met
at a fancy casino, where he is a waiter,
not the owner.

What good would it do me to disapprove?
As long as Violeta is hopeful, she is following
Ofelia's instructions about learning who
we really are
instead of allowing men
to train us.

HORSEPOWER

Poor Abuela hardly works anymore.
Arthritis curls her fingers.
Cars replace horses.
Las mambisas
will soon be forgotten
by young people who crave
roaring engines.

Fortunately, Maceo loves to ride bareback,
the two of us doubled up on Ala,
so that together we feel
like some sort of ancient miracle, a centaur
with three heads, four legs,
one
heart.

MACEO'S NAME

Lieutenant General José Antonio
de la Caridad Maceo y Grajales
was the most beloved officer
during the wars for independence.

Las mambisas called him the Bronze Titan
for his height, strength, and color, the same hue
as this new Maceo, my novio, with his parents
and grandparents
of various races.

Enemy soldiers called the first Maceo a lion
because of his courage.
Killed in battle, he is now remembered
as a martyr for the paired causes of freedom
for enslaved people and liberty from colonization
by Spain.

My novio Maceo's ancestors fought alongside him,
so the name was passed along as a tribute
to their sacrifice.

MAY 1928

Ofelia and her friends petition the government
to grant equal rights to all men and women.

Instead of agreeing, the tyrant gives himself
a new title: Illustrious and Exemplary Citizen.

The result is an outbreak of violence, with riots
and skirmishes, the threat of a real war growing
 closer
    and closer
        each
            night.

In the mornings, I always awaken
expecting news of some unimaginable
catastrophe.

OCTOBER 1929

The stock market crashes in New York,
and suddenly this whole island is poor.

Sugar prices tumble, farmers suffer,
every shopkeeper, factory worker,
and child
experiences
hunger.

NOVEMBER 1929

Despite the economic crisis, brave Ofelia
meets with Machado, demanding fulfillment
of his promise to give women the vote.

He refuses, and her petition for the rights
of natural children
fails too.

Disappointment.
Confusion.
Love.
Work.
All I can do is continue
on the path I've chosen,
delaying marriage until life
is normal.

A GLIMPSE OF HORROR

The beggar who comes to our door
does not resemble Violeta.

Ragged clothes, tangled hair, eyes as empty
as the space between stars . . .

Ayúdame, she pleads so quietly that my first thought
is just a whisper—has my sister become a rebel,
an enemy
of the tyrant
wanted by his
assassins?

But no, el tirano does not even know she exists.
The truth is far more personal and terrifying.
Her papá—my father—is the reason she wears
this disguise, so she can ask to hide here with me
until she can find a better place
to evade
legal murder.

FEMICIDE

My sister and her novio are both hiding
to avoid being shot or stabbed, after our father
discovered that she is carrying a child.

Is there any other situation where emotions
can be used as a valid defense in court?

If women could vote, no man would ever
be allowed to execute his pregnant daughter
and her lover just to protect his own
reputation.

HARBORING A FUGITIVE

Violeta and her novio fled
in different directions, each seeking
a separate place to hide.

Now I have to convince Mamá
that my half-sister deserves our protection.

Rich blue sky.
Golden wings.
How easy it is for me to daydream out loud
beneath stained-glass birds made by Maceo.

Somehow, I convince Mamá and Abuela
that Violeta should stay here with us, so I can be
the bearer of messages between her and the father
of her baby.

Surely las mambisas will gather around
like mounted angels, conspiring to protect
all of us.

MESSENGER

Galloping on Ala,
I reach a hut
in the green
glorious
countryside.

Exhausted, I return at a walk,
clutching a love note for my half-sister
from her novio.

The folded leaf of paper in my hand
feels as light and powerful as a feather
that floats down from the hopes
of a passing
dove.

SOUND

My father appears on his stallion,
first as a shadowy spy, then sunlit reality. . . .

He starts chasing me, so I press my knees
to Ala's sides, and even though she's tired,
her ears lie flat with rage
as she springs forward
carrying me away
from his threats.

He flourishes an old sword
and bellows the same word I remember
from childhood: ¡Bastarda!

No wonder I was always so fearful
of men and boys who echoed his insult!
No wonder I cringed every time he came
to our casa chica, leaving my mother bruised
and shaken by his violent objections
to her declarations of feminista
independencia.

PANIC ON HORSEBACK

My father's racehorse
closes the distance between us,
and even though he never actually
shouts that he'll kill me, the waving blade
of his heirloom sword
makes that statement
clearly.

Fright
unlike anything
I've experienced
since childhood
seizes my lungs,
forcing breath
into a whirlpool
of erratic
heartbeats.

But mambisas are brave,
so I gather my strength,
lean forward like a jockey
in a race, and plead with Dios
as I press Ala forward and up
over fences
ditches
streams. . . .

By the time I'm far enough ahead
to feel safe, I know I can't go home,
where that monster will find me
and punish me for helping
my sister
escape
legal
murder.

PART FIVE

DOWN WITH TYRANTS!

1930–1933

MY ESCAPE

I turn Ala loose, tell her to go home,
and quietly, stealthily, make my way
on foot, all the way to the city
of crowds and chaos.

Ofelia's friends help me find a printshop
where I can work, eat, and sleep surrounded
by nothing but words.

Here, I am safe from my father,
but I miss my mother and Abuela,
and I worry about Violeta.

Machado's guards could arrest me
at any moment, charging me
with revolutionary activity,
then hurling me off the seawall
into a thrashing mass
of sharks.

How will I ever manage to visit Maceo,
or invite him to visit me?

Sooner or later there will be a way,
but for now all I can do
is print, print, print. . . .

Oh, how I wish I could live two
parallel lives, one with my family
and my beloved, the other with
words
words
words
carefully designed
to recruit women
for the suffrage movement
and for the revolution against a dictator,
and for the cause of changing laws
that persecute children born beyond
the borders
of marriage.

ELECTRICITY

The city is a blaze of lights.
After a lifetime of moon, stars,
candles, and the soft flicker
of kerosene lanterns, these illuminated
streets are frightening, leaving me so far
from any shadowy place to hide
while I deliver poems of truth
to readers who dare
to question
the tyrant's
lies.

CIVIL WAR

The economic depression deepens.
Hardworking farmers and laborers starve
while foreign gangsters and corrupt politicians
show off illicit wealth, building ostentatious hotels
that overlook the sea, with peacocks strutting
beside fountains and movie stars luxuriating
in fancy casinos.

Street battles break out after dark,
clashes between Machado's assassins
and hordes of desperate students, workers,
artists, musicians, poets, feministas. . . .

Explosions, gunfire, funerals.
Each night of fighting leads us closer
to accepting constant violence
as normal.

I DREAM OF LOVE

Books are the only respite from war.
I read until I'm calm, typeset until I'm dizzy,
print until
hopeful
metaphors
and similes
replace
an endless
atmosphere
of terror.

In the end, all I'm left with is sleep
and the chance to dream of Maceo
for a few floating hours of imaginary
peace.

AWAKE

I remember that Maceo is not really with me.
I'm alone, separated from him by the need
to hide from my father.

Poor Violeta, I hope she is safe too.
How strange it seems to think of her
as vulnerable, after all the years I spent
assuming that wealth
could protect her.

If only women could gain true equality,
we would no longer be forced to survive
as fugitives from men who seek vengeance.
Ofelia tells me that each feminista must decide
whether to delay the struggle for suffrage, waiting
until Machado and his assassins have been overthrown,
but I cannot compromise. I need an end to both
forms of oppression, the wider tyranny
imposed by a cruel presidente
and legalized violence
within families.

Voting rights are our only
pathway to freedom from fear.

VISITATION

Somehow, Abuela has learned where I am.
She sneaks in the back door from an alley,
whispering quick promises to keep Violeta safe
by rallying las mambisas, who will move her
from house to house, out in remote farmlands.
My grandma has never been one to hide truths,
no matter how frightening, so she tells me
that my father barges into our house
night after night, hoping to interrogate me
so he can find
and execute
my half-sister.

Abuela smiles as she admits that he never
suspects that she, an old woman, and my mother,
his former mistress, might be Violeta's
real guardians.

PROPOSAL

Maceo is my next unexpected visitor.
He asks for my hand in marriage, and of course
I say ¡sí! because I love him, but I also answer
todavía no—not yet—because we both know
that first I need to hide and wait
until my whereabouts
are no longer
such a dangerous secret.

After he leaves, I plunge broken metal letters
into the printshop's fiery hellbox, an oven
where old words are melted and given new forms.

If only I could do the same with shattered fragments
of my life.

WE WERE TOGETHER FOR
JUST A FEW MINUTES . . .

but we breathed with a rhythm,
as if we were walking
outdoors
matching footsteps.

Now, soothed by that wisp of love
from last night,
I imagine that my midnight surroundings
are sunlit
instead of electrified.

Will I always have to choose the secrecy
of a fugitive
instead of accepting the open joy
of closeness?

MY GLASSY LIFE

Questioning my choices, I venture
onto the streets alone, feeling as wide
and transparent as a window—the wind's eye
a pathway for air and light to flow freely
unless it's covered with the sharp
hardness of glass.

Everyone around me rushes, oblivious
to my vulnerability, the printed posters and poems
that will make me a target of the tyrant's assassins
if I'm caught delivering rebellious words
to revolutionaries.

All it would take to shatter my wild vision of hope
is one brief encounter with a policeman
or soldier.

CLAMOR

Streetcars, automobiles, horns, bells,
rattling engines, moaning brakes,
and the hoof-drums of a lone mare
who dances as she shies and snorts,
startled by the noisy motion
of frantic traffic,
a plague of cacophony
that newspapers
call progress,
while to me
it simply looks
and sounds
like torment
for the eyes
and ears
of humans
and horses.

My anxious mind chooses to follow
the four-legged creature instead of cars
as I make my way through a crowd,
searching for places to display
prohibited posters.

¡Abajo! Surely anyone who sees
that printed word will sense

an unstated part of the slogan:
¡Abajo al tirano!
Down with the tyrant!

Silently, I pray that Machado's thugs
won't catch me accusing their boss
of being what he is: a bully.

NONVIOLENCE

Maybe I could try to fight with guns
like so many others.
Perhaps I'm a coward,
but wouldn't bullets be safe
compared to the dangers I face
while distributing posters?

Abajo.
Down.
It's a challenge.
Now all I have to do is wait for others
to put the same word on picket signs
and march, march, march, charging
along the streets in groups so huge
that no one can crush
our
power.

JUST WHEN I'M MOST IN NEED
OF ENCOURAGEMENT

Journalists finally take up Ofelia's debate
about the Adultery Law, filling newspaper pages
with history.

Women are property, reporters explain.
Wife-killing and daughter-murder are legal
only because colonial laws with medieval roots
persist, defended by men who benefit
from a convenient
injustice.

Now it's time for us—all women and girls—
to be treated like people,
not things.

Seeing Ofelia's words so clearly accepted
by reporters
makes me feel like my own voice
has finally
been heard.

OVERNIGHT, MY WHOLE WORLD CHANGES

The slaughter of wives
and daughters
along with their lovers
is suddenly outlawed!
And even though Machado
refuses to sign the bill,
he does not use his veto power,
so the new law passes,
making ancient rules
about fatherly
vengeance
obsolete.

I feel winged.
I can fly wherever I want,
leave this city, return to my home
and my novio, live without
fear.

DEFINITIONS

Women are no longer property,
but I'm still an illegitimate child
who does not exist in any archive
of my father's signed and stamped
official documents.

To him, natural
still means beastly,
an animal
hunted.

So despite the new law,
I'll have to remain
cautious.

DECLARATION

Women's suffrage.
Natural children's rights.
One legal victory makes these other needs
seem possible, so maybe I should stay here
in the city, in this printshop, working
toward freedom, spreading words
that sing and shout
as I demand
a chance
to speak out
by voting.

Will Maceo understand
if I delay marriage until he and I
are equals?

NOVEMBER 1930

Machado outlaws public gatherings
and suspends the constitution.

It's a crisis of unimaginable
helplessness.

Newspapers are censored,
then shut down, offices closed,
printing presses silenced.

Students are slaughtered by assassins.
Mothers who protest are killed by shots
"fired into the air."

Arrests.
Torture.
Disappearances.
The consequences of resisting
grow more and more perilous each day.

One brave woman even bares her shoulders
at a hearing in the House of Representatives,
to reveal bruises from beatings,
but her suffering is ignored
by powerful men who pretend
they don't believe her,

when the truth is they just
don't care.

Throughout all this turmoil, the tyrant continues
to insist that he's on the side of universal suffrage,
his promise of voting rights repeated often enough
to keep some feministas fooled.
Not me.
My only certainty is persistence.
For each of the dictator's lies,
I print and distribute
at least one
truth.

CHRISTMAS 1930

Maceo visits, his gift a kiss of patience
and this translucent glass nacimiento,
each shepherd, lamb, and member
of the Holy Family
glowing from within limbs
of breath-blown light.

My gift to Maceo is a promise
to keep working toward a world
where if we have a daughter
she will be equal and free.
Miraculously
        he agrees.

JANUARY 1931

We march, march, march,
every feminista from every voting club,
all of us united and fearless as we rally
in front of the tyrant's palace, shouting for him
to come out and meet us.

Arrogance convinces Machado that we must be
enthusiastic supporters hoping to greet him,
so he steps onto his balcony, waving proudly
to the crowd.

That is the moment when we unfurl banners
and raise protest signs high, boldly announcing
DOWN WITH TYRANTS! RESIGN EXECUTIVE POWER!
THE PEOPLE DEMAND IT!

Disbelief clouds the dictator's face as he turns away
from our challenge, nodding toward his guards
in a signal for the police to chase us.

Breathless and exhilarated
we escape.

FEBRUARY 1931

Machado's guards devise a scheme
for employing women to attack other women.

Stripped naked and raked with the metal fingernails
      of female bullies
         young feministas
            are terrorized.

The victims' fathers are too ashamed
of their daughters' humiliation
to press charges in court, so the thugs
feel triumphant . . .

but the next time it happens, male students devise
their own scheme: dressing as women to fool the police.

This time, attacks are met with punches
by men who have practiced boxing.

Perhaps we should all learn self-defense,
even those of us who are devoted
to nonviolence.

MARCH 1931

The government tries to silence us
by offering to appoint a woman
to a high position, but all
feminista organizations
unanimously oppose
any substitute
for suffrage,
so we
continue
to protest
and shout
hoping
our voices
will finally
be heard.

How long can this go on?
I don't care.
I'm determined.
Without justice, I have
nothing.

MARCH 1932

We've protested every day for a year,
until the chief justice of the Supreme Court
resigns in response to island-wide
lawlessness.

JUNE 1932

We publish
a list of congressmen
who continue to vote
against women's rights.

JULY 1932

Chaos!

¡EL MACHADATO!
1933

Warfare and hunger,
bodies rotting in the street,
and now the United States
threatens to invade,
making everything
so intolerable
that finally
the tyrant
is overthrown
by his own soldiers.

The leader of the coup is an officer
named Fulgencio Batista y Zaldívar,
but he does not become el presidente—not yet.
For now, the first interim ruler of Cuba is someone
who lasts only one month, quickly followed
by another, Dr. Ramón Grau San Martín,
a favorite of students, workers,
and feministas.
El Dr. Grau
gives us
hope.

SUFFRAGE AT LAST
1934

Grau grants women the right to vote!
Triumph for all of us!
For las mambisas
who fought so hard, so long ago
and for their great-granddaughters
not yet born,
one generation after another,
with every girl growing up
as her brother's
true equal.

No more struggling to convince men
that women are not biologically inferior
or otherwise unable to make wise decisions
at the ballot box
in elections
that will determine
the safety and well-being of families.

Celebration is too mild a term for this feeling.
There is nothing more festive
than a sigh
of relief.

INTERFERENCE FROM THE
NORTHERN BULLY

Trouble confronts us almost immediately.
Unable to accept the prospect of a free Cuba,
the United States refuses to recognize Dr. Grau,
so he falls from power, taking with him
our female victory.

The next few presidentes all turn out to be
very temporary, and each one must be convinced
that women should be able to vote,
so our petitions seem endless,
like the fairy-tale task of spinning
and weaving brittle straw
into gleaming gold.

Brave girls.
Impossible odds.
We face our future
over and over
in so many real
and imaginary
ways.

BY THE TIME I FINALLY RETURN HOME
1935

I discover that Mamá and Abuela have moved
to a new house they built with money from
their combined modern pharmacy
and traditional herbal medicine
business, a shop that fills
the lower floor, while our rooms
are perched above, the angel-bird windows
from our old broken-stone home
now displayed along with scraps of lace,
rusty horseshoes, and a feeling
made of freedom's airy
light.

INDEPENDENCIA

We are not squatters here.
This property belongs to us,
not my father.

No one can tell us to leave.
Even Violeta and her husband
are free now, because she
has been disowned
and disinherited,
so she's learning to work
as a seamstress, earning
her own money to support
their child, a cheerful girl
who follows Abuela around
as she feeds, grooms, and rides
our horses, the legacy of mounted
mambisa
pride.

I don't know who makes me happier,
Maceo or Ala, because both feel like parts
of my true self, the independent woman
who has overcome such deeply
piercing fears.

I'm no longer frightened by men and boys.

I don't get breathless or feel weak enough
to faint, not even on Sundays when I sit
in church, where my father glares at me
as if he still imagines that I am his property.

One person.
One vote.
I am
not
an object.
I am human.

ELECTIONS
1936

¡VIVA!
Las mambisas gather on horseback,
young and old, all of us exuberant
as we prance to the polling place,
ready to cast the first female votes
on this island of hope.

My baby rides within me,
my husband smiling
from the roadside,
where supporters
of women's rights
cheer as we dismount
for our moment of joy.

Mamá is not just voting;
she's also a candidate for our local
municipal council, running against the man
who refused to marry her when I was a baby—
my father, whose corruption and violent temper
make Mamá a favorite in all the newspapers,
especially the new one
that I own, edit, and print.

Will she win?
Perhaps, but even if she loses,

there will be other elections
with members of all the voting clubs
now running
running
running
until women
who practiced
independence
by galloping
sidesaddle
can sit forward
facing our future
as we finally
finish claiming
exhilarating
equality.

¡Vivan las mambisas!
Life to old rebels
and young!

HISTORICAL NOTE

This book is a work of historical fiction. Rima and her family are imaginary characters, but the feministas like Ofelia, and the facts surrounding their struggle for women's rights, are all thoroughly documented.*

Beginning in the 1800s and continuing beyond the 1930s, many Cuban feminists paired a demand for suffrage with other social justice issues. One of the most essential was the campaign to end the archaic Adultery Law, which permitted men to kill unfaithful wives and disobedient daughters, along with the women's lovers. Adultery was prohibited only for women. It was common for men to keep mistresses in las casas chicas (small houses).

The vast majority of illegitimate ("natural") children were mixed-race, with varying degrees of African, Indigenous, and Chinese ancestry. They were not entitled to share their fathers' surnames and inheritances, or to receive any financial or emotional support during childhood. These children and their mothers were often impoverished, shunned, and insulted, both by the church and by neighbors. Unmarried mothers depended on the generosity of relatives, until job training programs organized by feminists provided dignity and an escape from poverty. Illegitimate children finally received partial equality in 1940.

Even though Cuban women were officially granted suffrage in 1934, the first election where they were able to vote did not occur until 1936. During that historic election, women not only voted, but some also ran for office, realizing the dream of their mambisa predecessors who fought for independence from Spain, freedom from slavery, and a hopeful future.

Tragically, Fulgencio Batista y Zaldívar, the military officer who helped lead a coup against the dictator Gerardo Machado y Morales, later became a dictator himself. Batista was overthrown by Fidel Castro Ruz, who also became a dictator. Throughout all the challenges of the island's turbulent history, many women have remained brave and influential, continuing the struggle for full equality.

*The most comprehensive reference is:

Stoner, K. Lynn. *From the House to the Streets: The Cuban Women's Movement for Legal Reform, 1898-1940*. Durham: Duke University Press. 1991.

INTERNATIONAL TIMELINE OF WOMEN'S SUFFRAGE

Asterisks indicate partial voting rights rather than complete.

PRE-1600S: IROQUOIS AND MANY OTHER
      INDIGENOUS NATIONS
1838: PITCAIRN
1881: ISLE OF MAN
1893: NEW ZEALAND
1894: AUSTRALIA*
1906: FINLAND
1913: NORWAY
1915: DENMARK
1917: URUGUAY, RUSSIA
1918: GREAT BRITAIN*, GERMANY, CANADA*
1919: NETHERLANDS, SWEDEN*, AFGHANISTAN*
1920: UNITED STATES*, BELGIUM*
1930: SOUTH AFRICA*
1931: SPAIN*
1932: BRAZIL*, THAILAND
1934: CUBA*
1937: PHILIPPINES
1942: DOMINICAN REPUBLIC
1944: FRANCE
1946: VENEZUELA, VIETNAM
1947: ARGENTINA, CHINA, INDIA
1950: HAITI
1951: NEPAL
1953: MEXICO*
1954: COLOMBIA, GHANA, NIGERIA*
1955: CAMBODIA, ETHIOPIA, NICARAGUA, PERU
1956: EGYPT
1960: BAHAMAS
1963: KENYA, MOROCCO
1965: BOTSWANA
1971: SWITZERLAND
2015: SAUDI ARABIA

Dates shown in this timeline are just overall examples. Many of the world's 195 countries have complex histories with fluctuations in voting rights. In some nations, such as Sweden, single women with property were allowed to vote much earlier than married women. In other countries, including Nigeria and Mexico, voting rights were initially regional, depending on limitations imposed by men within local religious and ethnic groups. In parts of Sierra Leone, and in the US state of New Jersey, women voted long before the general female populations of the nations where they were located.

Countries with a colonial history have often based voting rights for all genders on discriminatory racial policies. In Australia, Indigenous people were not free to vote until 1962. In South Africa, White and Asian women gained suffrage long before Black women. Canada did not allow Indigenous people of any gender to vote until 1960, unless they renounced allegiance to their own First Nations. In the United States, Indigenous voting rights for all genders varied from state to state until 1957. In addition, Asian Americans of all genders did not gain full suffrage in the United States until 1952. African Americans and Mexican Americans of all genders were often intimidated or kept away from elections until after the Voting Rights Act of 1965. Even now, corrupt politicians in the United States continue attempting to suppress voting rights through gerrymandering and other racist schemes.

All over the world, the freedom to vote can be abruptly cut off by any dictatorship, either because no elections are held, candidates run unopposed, or citizens are punished for voting against a tyrant. For instance, Spaniards lost voting rights under Franco and did not regain them until after his death. Protecting suffrage requires constant vigilance in every nation. Voting for candidates and policies that protect people and resources is one of the few ways we can ensure that our future is hopeful.

ACKNOWLEDGMENTS

I thank God for the perseverance of nonviolent activists who struggle for freedom on so many levels.

I am profoundly grateful to my husband, Curtis Engle, our family, friends, and colleagues. I'm grateful to my mamá and my abuela for assuring me that I could be anything I wanted, even a poet.

Special thanks to my wonderful agent, Michelle Humphrey; my superb editor, Reka Simonsen; and the entire marvelous Atheneum publishing team.